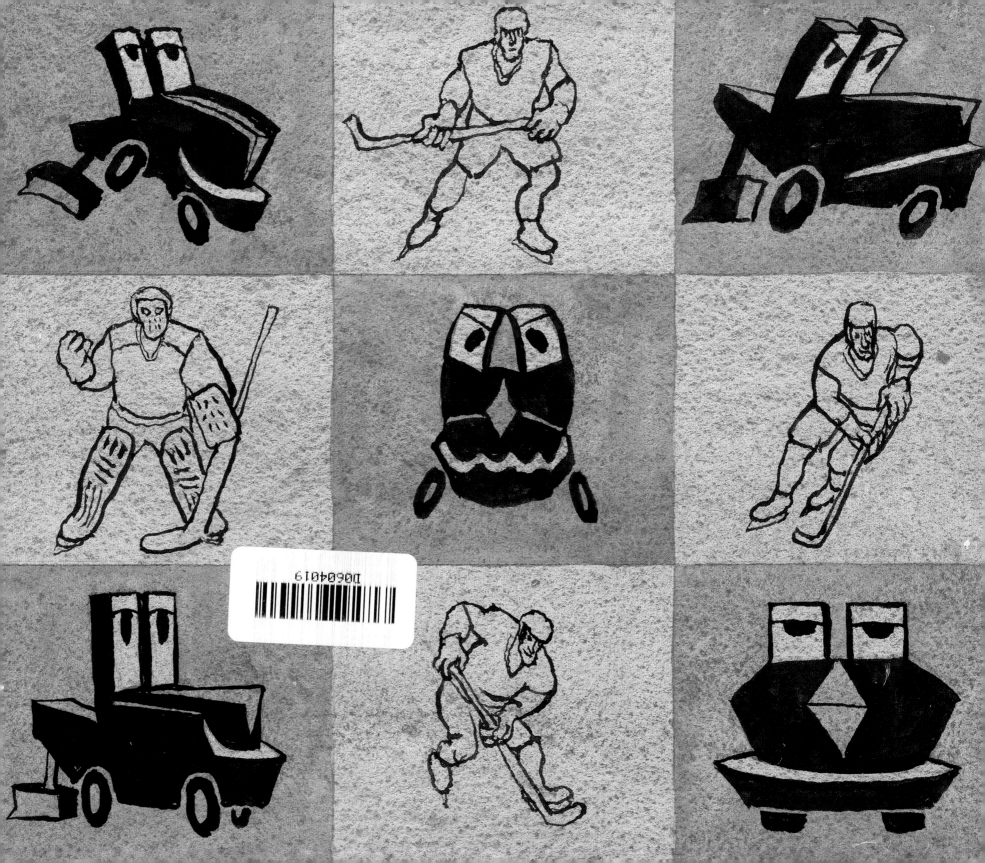

COOLEST JOB
in the world,
right here, baby.

3...
2...
1...

BUZZZZZZZZZZZZZZZZZZZZZZZZ!

Wheeling down the home stretch, belly full of SNOW, countin' down the tick-tock:

AROUND and AROUND

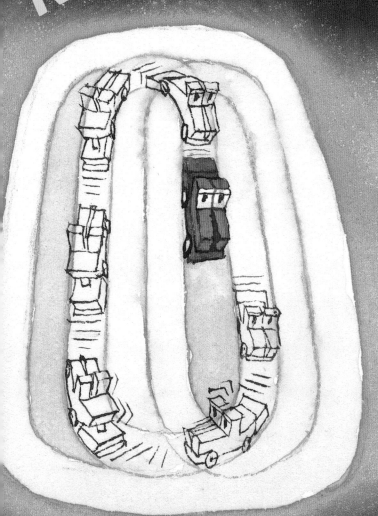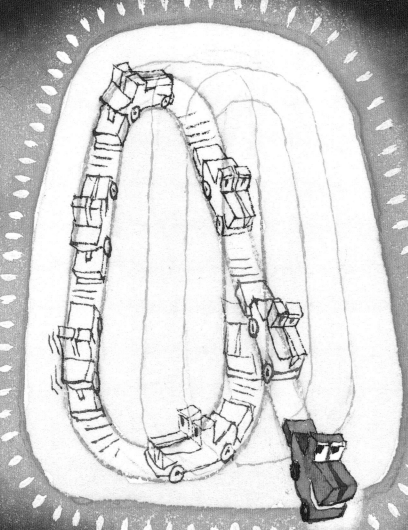

and AROUND and AROUND I GO,

'til the whole rink's S-M-O-O-T-H as glass.

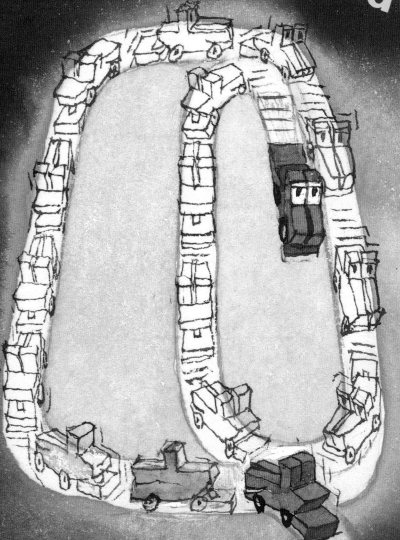

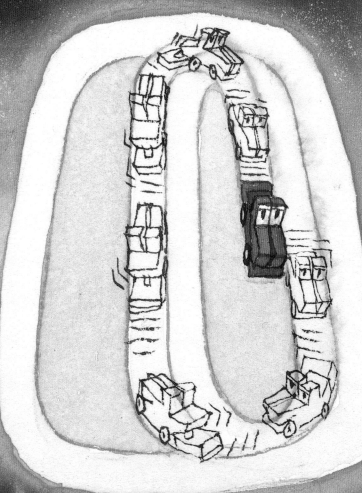

Even if you know
how a bumblebee flies
or a spider spins her web,
IT'S STILL MAGIC.

Warm-water pipe,
SPRRRRRRITZ!
Fill up the DENTS and PITS and RUTS.

Towel,
S-P-R-E-A-D the water O-U-T.

Water,
FREEZE
into fresh, slick ice.

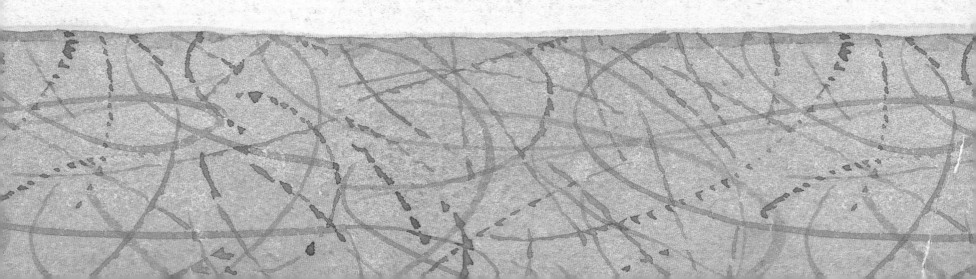

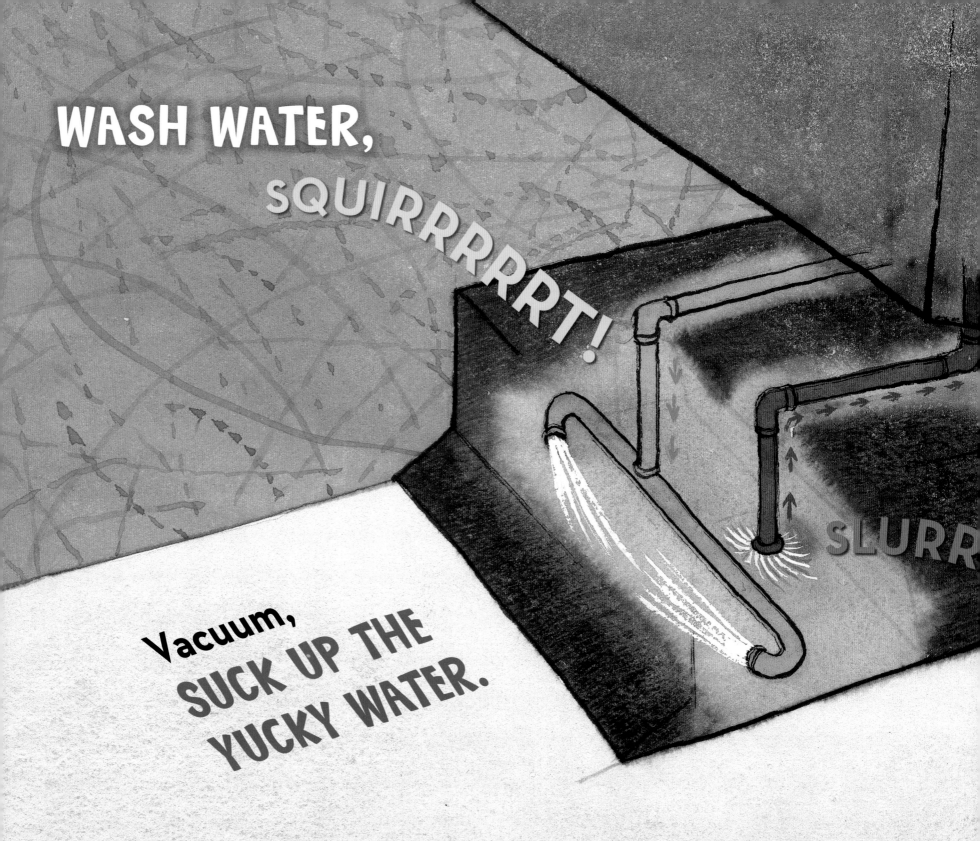

Blade?

SHAVE THE ICE—

VZZZZZZZZZZZT!

AND MAKE IT SNOW!

Level auger?

SPIN SNOW TO CENTER.

Tall auger?

WHIRL IT UP.

How do I do it?
Crank up your X-ray vision
and I'll SHOW ya how!

Rough ice in front of me . . .

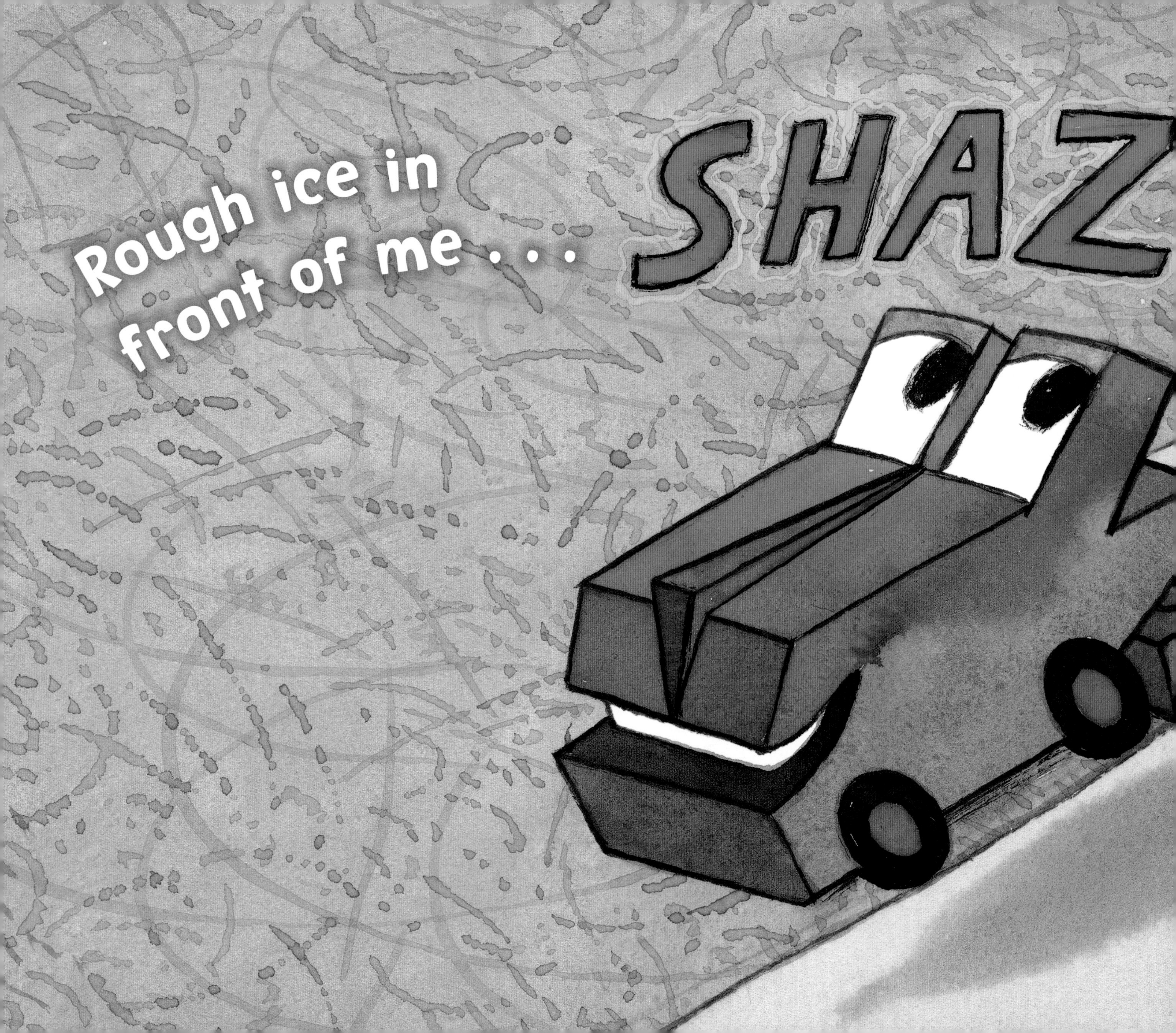

ZAMBONI MACHINE, YA
MOVE LIKE A TURTLE.
LOOK—THE CLOCK'S TICKING!
HIT THE GAS! FINISH UP
SO WE CAN GET BACK TO THE GAME!

Not so fast, Big Talker.
Gotta check the damages.
Look at those DENTS and PITS and RUTS.

The rougher the ice,
the deeper I shave.

'Cause I'm a

blade-packing, ice-shaving,

snow-eating,

water-spraying,

For our grandson, Arthur James Abramson

MANY THANKS TO ALL THE COOL
PEOPLE WHO HELPED US WITH THIS BOOK:
David Meltzer, Operations Director of Central Park's Wollman Rink,
Neil Walsh of New York City's Sky Rink, Frank J. Zamboni & Co., Inc.,
and Adam Abramson, Senior Technical Adviser.

THANKS TO THE HARPERCOLLINS CREW:
Hadley Dyer, Alessandra Balzer, Kelsey Murphy, Dana Fritts,
Ruiko Tokunaga, and Kathryn Silsand, and to the team at Pippin Properties:
Holly McGhee, Michael Steiner, Elena Giovinazzo, and Courtney Stevenson.

...WHOA!
HE'S DOWN!
HE'S DOWN!
OOH,
that's GOTTA hurt.
Nobody can skate
on ice this rough.
I mean
NOBODY!

ZAMBONI and the configuration
of the Zamboni® ice resurfacing machine are
registered in the U.S. Patent and Trademark Office as the
trademarks of Frank J. Zamboni & Co., Inc.

Balzer + Bray is an imprint of HarperCollins Publishers.

I'm Cool!
Text copyright © 2015 by Kate McMullan · Illustrations copyright © 2015 by Jim McMullan
Library of Congress Control Number: 2014947373
ISBN 978-0-06-230629-6

The artist used watercolor and gouache to create the illustrations for this book.
16 17 18 19 SCP 10 9 8 7 6 5 4 3 2 ❖ First Edition

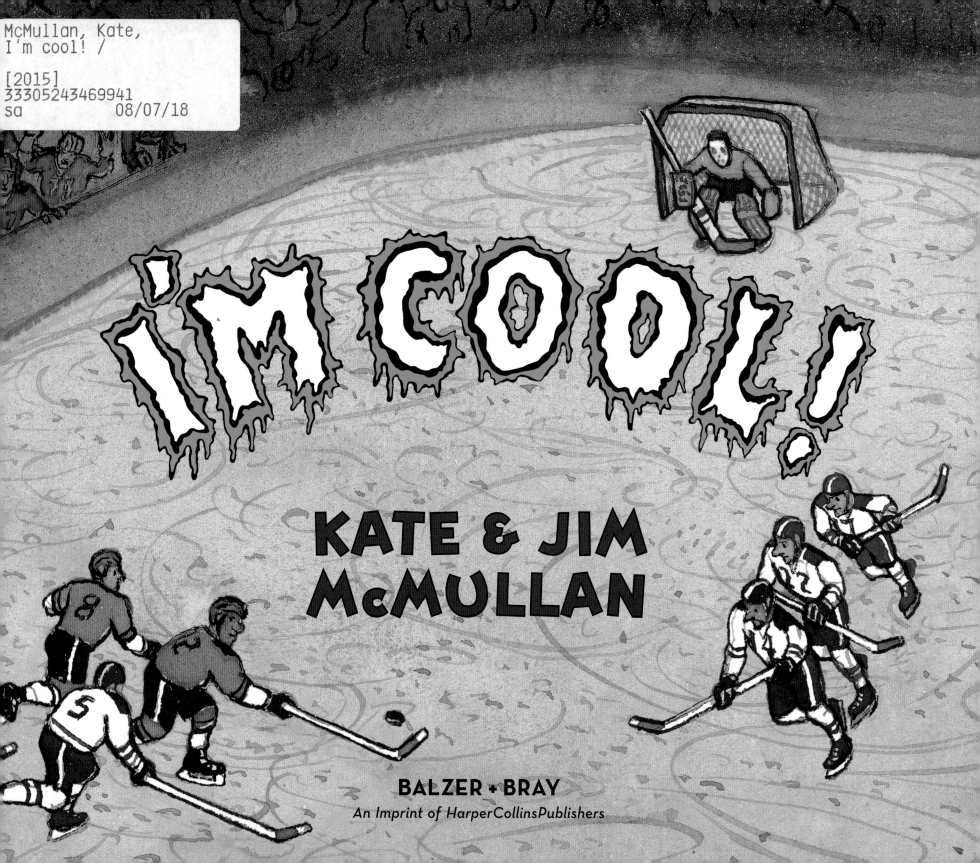

¡'M COOL!

KATE & JIM McMULLAN

BALZER + BRAY

An Imprint of HarperCollinsPublishers

TIGERS 2
POLAR BEARS 2

Game's tied in
the first period.
HERE'S THE FACE-OFF.
A Tiger player gains control
of the puck. He's skating
for the Polar Bear
goal . . .